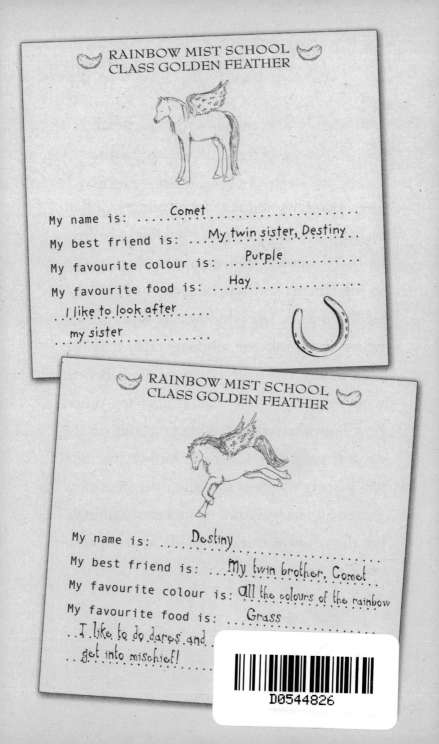

RAINBOW MIST SCHOOL
CLASS GOLDEN FEATHER

My name is: Comet

My best friend is: My twin sister, Destiny

My favourite colour is: Purple

My favourite food is: Hay

I like to look after my sister

RAINBOW MIST SCHOOL
CLASS GOLDEN FEATHER

My name is: Destiny

My best friend is: My twin brother, Comet

My favourite colour is: All the colours of the rainbow

My favourite food is: Grass

I like to do dares and get into mischief!

D0544826

Sue Bentley's books for children often include animals, fairies and wildlife. She lives in Northampton and enjoys reading, going to the cinema and watching the birds on the feeders outside her window. She loves horses, which she thinks are all completely magical. One of her favourite books is *Black Beauty*, which she must have read at least ten times. At school she was always getting told off for daydreaming, but she now knows that she was storing up ideas for when she became a writer. Sue has met and owned many animals, but the wild creatures in her life hold a special place in her heart.

Sue Bentley

A Special Wish

Illustrated by Angela Swan

PUFFIN

To Champion — wonderful and steadfast

PUFFIN BOOKS

Published by the Penguin Group
Penguin Books Ltd, 80 Strand, London WC2R 0RL, England
Penguin Group (USA) Inc., 375 Hudson Street, New York, New York 10014, USA
Penguin Group (Canada), 90 Eglinton Avenue East, Suite 700, Toronto, Ontario, Canada M4P 2Y3
(a division of Pearson Penguin Canada Inc.)
Penguin Ireland, 25 St Stephen's Green, Dublin 2, Ireland (a division of Penguin Books Ltd)
Penguin Group (Australia), 250 Camberwell Road, Camberwell, Victoria 3124, Australia
(a division of Pearson Australia Group Pty Ltd)
Penguin Books India Pvt Ltd, 11 Community Centre, Panchsheel Park, New Delhi – 110 017, India
Penguin Group (NZ), 67 Apollo Drive, Rosedale, North Shore 0632, New Zealand
(a division of Pearson New Zealand Ltd)
Penguin Books (South Africa) (Pty) Ltd, 24 Sturdee Avenue, Rosebank,
Johannesburg 2196, South Africa

Penguin Books Ltd, Registered Offices: 80 Strand, London WC2R 0RL, England

puffinbooks.com

First published 2009
1

Text copyright © Sue Bentley, 2009
Illustrations copyright © Angela Swan, 2009
All rights reserved

The moral right of the author and illustrator has been asserted

Set in Bembo
Made and printed in England by Clays Ltd, St Ives plc

British Library Cataloguing in Publication Data
A CIP catalogue record for this book is available from the British Library

ISBN: 978-0-141-32594-1

Mixed Sources
Product group from well-managed
forests and other controlled sources
www.fsc.org Cert no. SA-COC-1592
© 1996 Forest Stewardship Council

Penguin Books is committed to a sustainable future
for our business, our readers and our planet.
The book in your hands is made from paper
certified by the Forest Stewardship Council.

Prologue

Comet tried to squash a small flutter of hope as he flew back towards his magical island home. 'Destiny must be home safely by now!' the young magic pony cried. His twin sister had been lost for so long.

Spreading his gold-feathered wings, he soared downwards, speeding across the wide sea and galloping over the crests of the waves. Soon, Rainbow Mist Island came into view. Its mountains and forests were almost hidden in softly shimmering, multicoloured clouds that gave the island its name. Comet's heart lifted. It felt good to be home.

The magic pony drifted over the shore. Rainbow droplets gleamed like jewels on his cream coat and flowing golden mane and tail. Moments later, he touched down on to the grass of a small clearing.

Tossing his head, Comet looked about warily at the huge trees that grew all around, their glowing leaves tinkling faintly. He could feel no trace of the dark horses who wanted to steal his magic.

As the magic pony snorted with satisfaction, there was a movement and an older horse with a wise expression stepped forward.

'Blaze!' Comet bent his neck in a bow before the leader of the Lightning Herd.

Blaze's dark eyes softened with affection. 'I am pleased to see you again, Comet. But where is Destiny?' he asked in a deep gentle voice.

'She is not here? Then she is still in danger!' Comet whinnied sadly.

Destiny had playfully borrowed the Stone of Power, which protected the Lightning Herd from the dark horses, but the stone was accidentally lost while the twin magic ponies were playing cloud-chase. Comet later found the stone but before he could tell Destiny, she ran away, thinking she was in lots of trouble.

'My sister still thinks she has put the Lightning Herd in danger and cannot forgive herself,' Comet explained to the older horse. A lump rose in his throat as he realized that his twin sister was still alone and in hiding far from home.

Blaze shook his wise old head slowly. 'You must go after her again, my young friend. Find Destiny and tell her that the Stone of Power is safe and bring her home.'

Comet's deep violet eyes flashed. He lifted his head. 'I will leave at once!'

'Wait!' Blaze ordered. Stamping his foot, he pawed at the grass. A fiery opal, swirling with flashes of rainbow light, appeared. 'The stone will help you to find her.'

The magic pony drew closer to the Stone of Power. A tremor passed over his pale silky coat as he peered deeply into the rainbow depths. The stone grew larger

4

and rays of dazzling light spread outwards.

An image formed in the centre. Comet gasped as he saw Destiny galloping across a green hillside beneath an open blue sky, in a world far away.

'I have to find her!' he whinnied.

There was a bright flash of dazzling violet light, and rainbow mist surrounded Comet. The cream-coloured pony, with his flowing golden mane and tail, and gleaming gold-feathered wings, disappeared. In his place there stood an elegant Connemara pony with a dapple-grey coat, a darker grey mane and tail and glowing deep violet eyes.

'There is no time to lose. Go now,' Blaze urged. 'Use this disguise. Find your twin sister and return with her safely.'

'I will!' Comet vowed.

The dapple-grey pony's coat ignited with violet sparks. Comet snorted as he felt the power building inside him. The shimmering rainbow mist swirled faster and faster and drew Comet in . . .

Chapter
ONE

Marcie Locket felt her heart beat faster
as she stood at the bottom of her garden,
looking over the fence into the adjoining
field. There was a big old shed to one side
– just perfect for a stable and storeroom.
Her new pony was going to love its
paddock!

Marcie beamed as she imagined all the
fun she would have looking after a pony

of her own. It was going to be brilliant to go out hacking whenever she liked. She might even get her dad to help her put a course of jumps up in the field.

'Marcie! Where are you?' her mum called impatiently. 'We need to go. I'll be waiting for you in the car.'

'Just coming!' Marcie answered.

Whirling round, she headed up the garden and into the house. The front door slammed shut behind her as she hurried out to the front drive.

'Sorry, Mum!' Bouncing into the front seat, Marcie dumped her school bag in the footwell and fastened her seat belt.

'Hmm. I don't need three guesses to know where you've been,' Mrs Locket said, smiling sideways at her as she waited for a gap in the traffic before pulling out.

Marcie smiled back, her eyes glowing with happiness. 'When's Dad going to hear about his job promotion?' she asked. He had promised that Marcie could have her pony once his new job was confirmed.

'I think he should be hearing by the end of the day,' her mum replied.

'Great! We can start looking at ponies for sale. It's Friday today, so we've got the whole weekend,' Marcie said excitedly. But then she sighed as she thought about her best friend who had recently moved away. 'I wish Lara was still here. She had loads of pony magazines. We could have looked through them to help me decide what sort of pony I want.'

'You're really missing her, aren't you? It's a shame she had to move so far away. But you both promised to keep in touch by phone and email, didn't you? And Lara can always come to stay in the school holidays,' Mrs Locket added.

Marcie knew her mum was right, but at that moment it didn't make her feel much better.

It wasn't going to be the same without her best friend living just around the corner. Marcie and Lara had known each other since they were in Reception class and had always sat together as they moved up the school. They used to spend every weekend together, taking it in turns to ride Lara's pony, Tramp.

'Lara's bound to forget all about me,' Marcie said glumly. 'She'll be busy making friends and riding ponies with them.'

'I'm sure she'll remember her old friends too,' her mum chided gently. 'And don't forget, there'll be a brand-new reason why Lara will be delighted to come and visit.'

'Oh yeah! My new pony!' Marcie exclaimed, starting to cheer up a bit again. 'Lara will want to know everything about it and she'll be dying to ride it.'

As they drove through the busy streets, Marcie let her thoughts wander, picturing ponies of every breed and colour imaginable. There were so many gorgeous ones out there. Where would they buy hers from? What was she going to call him or her?

They reached the school and Mum dropped her at the gates. Marcie gave her a kiss and waved as she drove away.

Marcie wandered into school in a daze – all she could think about was her new pony!

When she got to her usual desk by the window, she found Jessica Evans already sitting there. Jessica looked up and smiled as Marcie sat down. 'Hi, Marcie. Miss told me to sit here. I'm your new desk-buddy!'

Marcie smiled. 'Um . . . hi, Jessica. Fine by me.' She didn't mind Jessica at all but no one could ever replace Lara.

As the rest of the class filed in and took their seats, Jessica began telling Marcie about the new computer game she'd had for her birthday.

'It's got a brilliant console. I was playing games with my brother all last night and I got a really high score! He was dead jealous. What did you do?' she asked.

'I put a bits 'n' bridles poster up in my bedroom. It's got all the different types, like snaffle bits and flash nosebands,' Marcie began enthusiastically. 'I'm getting a pony of my own really soon, so I'm thinking about getting new tack for it . . .' She stopped as she noticed a glazed expression settle on Jessica's face.

'I just don't get ponies and riding at all,' Jessica commented. 'I mean, what's the big deal about galloping through muddy fields and stuff and getting freezing cold? Then you have to get up early to clean out pongy old messy stables and build muck heaps, don't you?'

'Well, yes,' Marcie admitted. 'But I like the smell of horses and there's other stuff to do that's lots of fun. It's all part of looking after your pony.'

Jessica widened her eyes incredulously. 'Fun? I'd rather hang upside down in custard. I'll stick to my computer games, thanks.'

'Right.' Marcie didn't know quite what else to say. A small wave of loneliness washed over her and she realized that she was missing Lara more than ever.

The rest of the day seemed to drag on forever and Marcie was relieved when the bell went for the end of lessons. The moment Miss Slater dismissed the class she grabbed her school bag and raced outside to meet her mum.

'Did Dad text you?' she asked eagerly as they drove home.

Mrs Locket shook her head. 'There's no news yet. You'll have to be patient for once. Although I know that's not your strong point!' she said, laughing.

Marcie grinned. 'Impatient? Me?!'

When they got home, Marcie skipped upstairs to change out of her school clothes. She was just doing up her jeans, when she heard the front door. Her dad was home! Dashing out of her room, she shot back down the stairs, two steps at a time.

'Hi, Dad!' Marcie sang, looking up at him excitedly. She stopped; why did he have such a serious look on his face? Today was a good day for all of them!

'Hello, love.' Mr Locket hung up his jacket and then ran his fingers through his short brown hair. 'Where's your mum?'

'Um . . . in the kitchen making supper, I think,' Marcie said, starting to feel that something was wrong.

She went and stood next to her mum

as Dad sat down at the table and began speaking. 'I'm afraid it's bad news. We were all called into a meeting late this afternoon, and told that the company's closing down,' he explained. 'I'm going to have to find another job. And to be honest, as things are at the moment, that could take some time.'

'Oh dear. That's quite a shock.' Mrs Locket sank on to a kitchen chair next to her husband and took his hand. 'Well, we'll manage. We'll just have to make cutbacks,' she decided firmly.

Marcie's heart sank. Something as expensive as a pony would definitely be one of the cutbacks her mum was talking about. But she bit her lip as she looked at Dad. He seemed pale and tense, although he was trying hard to put on a brave face.

She felt really bad for him.

Marcie went and gave both of her
parents a hug. 'I'm really sorry about your
job, Dad. And I can wait a bit longer for
my pony.'

'Thanks, love. That's my grown-up girl.'
Her dad hugged her back and dropped
a kiss on the top of her head. 'And don't
you worry. You mum and I will work this
out.'

Marcie nodded. She could tell that
they had lots to talk about. 'I think I'll . . .
um . . . go and sit in the garden . . . or
something,' she said.

Her mum nodded absently.

Marcie went outside and trudged down
to the paddock. She sighed as she thought
that it could be empty for quite a while.
If only Lara was here. Marcie could

have gone over to her house for a long
comforting talk.

Suddenly, there was a movement from
over near the old shed.

Marcie's eyes widened in surprise as
a dapple-grey pony with a darker grey

mane and tail appeared from behind it
and began walking towards her.

'Can you help me, please?' it asked in a
velvety neigh.

Chapter
TWO

'Oh!' Marcie did a double take.

She swallowed hard as she gazed at the pony in utter astonishment. What was going on? Had her mum and dad bought it as a surprise?

But how could they have done, when her dad had just lost his job?

Marcie couldn't work out why there was a pony in her paddock. And her imagination was obviously working overtime, because she'd just imagined that it had spoken to her!

As the pony leaned forward, Marcie reached a hand towards it. It had a short elegant head with a slightly dished nose and unusually large eyes. They were a stunning deep violet colour and glowed like amethysts.

She had never seen or heard of any pony with eyes like that before.

'Hello,' she breathed softly, letting it snuffle her to get her scent. 'You're absolutely gorgeous. You look like a Connemara pony. But however did you get in here?'

'I have just arrived from far away. My name is Comet of the Lightning Herd. What is yours?' asked the pony.

Marcie dropped her hand in shock and took two paces backwards. This pony really *had* just spoken to her. This couldn't be happening! Talking ponies only existed in fairy tales!

But the beautiful pony twitched his ears forward and stood looking at her calmly as if waiting for a reply to his question.

'I'm Marcie,' she gulped when she could speak again. 'Marcie Locket. I live here with my parents.'

Comet dipped his head in a bow. 'I am honoured to meet you, Marcie,' he said politely.

'Um . . . me too,' Marcie blurted out. She recalled something the pony had just said. 'What's . . . the Lightning Herd?'

'We are a family of horses who live on Rainbow Mist Island,' Comet told her proudly. 'Our leader is wise and strong. He is called Blaze. A Stone of Power protects our herd from the dark horses who would like to steal our magic.'

Marcie listened hard, still having trouble taking all this in.

'So why are you *here*?' she asked him.

Comet gave a soft blow. 'My twin sister,

Destiny, lost the Stone of Power when we were cloud-racing. I found it and it is safe again, but Destiny does not know this. She thought she was in terrible trouble for losing the stone, so she ran away to hide in your world. I have come here to look for her.'

Marcie's curiosity seemed to be getting the better of her shock. 'You and your twin sister were *cloud-racing*? But how . . .'

Comet backed away from the fence. 'I will show you. Stay there,' he neighed gently.

Marcie felt a strange warm tingling sensation flow to the very tips of her fingers as violet sparkles bloomed in Comet's dapple-grey coat and a veil of shimmering rainbow mist surrounded him.

The grey pony disappeared and in its
place stood a magnificent young cream-
coloured pony, with a flowing gold mane
and tail. Springing from his shoulders

were powerful wings, covered with gleaming golden feathers.

'Oh wow!' Marcie gasped, absolutely spellbound. The winged pony was the most beautiful thing she had ever seen. She caught her breath. 'C–Comet?'

'Yes, Marcie. It is still me,' Comet said in a deep musical whinny.

But before she could get used to the sight of Comet in his true form there was a final swirl of glittering rainbow mist and Comet reappeared as a handsome dapple-grey Connemara pony.

'That's a really cool disguise! Can Destiny use her magic to disguise herself too?' Marcie asked.

Comet nodded. 'But that will not save her from the dark horses if they discover her. She is in danger. I need to find

her and take her back to the safety of
Rainbow Mist Island. Will you help me,
Marcie?'

Marcie saw that Comet's deep violet
eyes were shadowed by worry for his
sister and her heart melted. 'Of course I
will. Oh, just wait until I write to my best
friend Lara about you.'

Comet swished his dark grey tail. 'I am
sorry, but you can tell no one about me
and what I have told you!'

Marcie was disappointed. She would
have loved to share this amazing secret
with Lara. It would have been very
special, more than ever with Lara living so
far away now.

'You must promise,' Comet said,
looking at her with his big eyes.

Marcie nodded slowly. If it would help

protect his twin sister from the dark
horses until Comet could find her, she
was prepared to agree. 'I promise. No
one's going to hear anything about you
and Destiny from me.'

'Thank you, Marcie.'

Reaching forward, Comet gently

bumped his nose against Marcie's arm.
She reached up to pat his satiny cheek.

'Marcie? Are you still down there?'
called a voice.

Marcie stiffened as she looked back at
the big flowering bushes that screened
the field from the house. She caught a
glimpse of her mum's bright blue top
through a small gap in the leaves.

'Mum's coming!' she gasped in panic.

Oh no! There wasn't time for her to
hide Comet. Her mum was going to
see her new magical pony friend at any
second!

What was she going to do?

Chapter
THREE

'There you are, love,' Mrs Locket said, slipping her arm round Marcie's shoulder as she came and stood beside her at the fence. 'I thought I'd find you here, staring at that rickety old shed we were going to turn into a stable. I hope you're not too upset about having to wait for your pony.'

'Um . . . well, I am a b–bit disappointed,' Marcie stammered. Why didn't her mum say anything about the gorgeous dapple-grey pony that was standing in the field as large as life?! Instead, Mum was just looking back at her in concern — it was almost as if she couldn't see Comet.

Marcie carried on carefully. 'I don't feel all that bad. It's not as if I'm never going to be able to have one, is it?' She was surprised to find that now Comet had arrived, she really was OK about having to wait for a pony of her own.

'Thanks for being so understanding, Marcie. Your dad's taken it quite hard,' Mrs Locket said. She sighed. 'I just hope it won't be too long before he finds work again.'

'It won't be. I've got a good feeling about it,' Marcie said.

'I hope you're right.' Her mum smiled
and reached out to ruffle Marcie's
shoulder-length brown hair. 'Well
– supper's almost ready. I'm just about to
dish it out. Are you coming in?'

Marcie looked at Comet, who
was listening to the conversation, his
intelligent eyes twinkling. It was really

odd. But Mrs Locket *still* didn't seem to have noticed him.

'Marcie?'

Marcie's head snapped back. 'I'll just be a minute.'

'Right you are.' Her mum turned and went back up the garden.

Marcie waited until she was out of sight behind the bushes before talking to Comet. 'I don't get it. What just happened?'

'I used my magic so that only you can hear and see me,' Comet told her.

'Really?' Marcie was delighted. 'So you're invisible now? That's really cool.' She had a sudden idea. 'Why don't you live in this paddock? No one will know except me. There's lots of juicy grass to eat, rainwater in the trough and the shed for shelter if it rains. And I'll come and see you whenever I can!'

Comet nodded. 'This is a good place to stay while I am searching for Destiny.'

'That's settled then,' Marcie said happily. 'I'd better go now, or Mum and Dad will wonder what's keeping me. I'll sneak out to see you later.'

'Thank you, Marcie.' Comet turned and walked a few steps, then bent his head and began cropping the grass with his strong young teeth.

After a final glance over her shoulder, Marcie hurried back up the garden. There was a brand-new pony in her paddock after all! But never in her wildest dreams could she have imagined that it would be one as amazing and magical as Comet!

*

Marcie was almost too excited to eat, but she made herself take her time. She didn't want her mum and dad thinking she had tummy ache and making her lie down for a rest.

After they finished supper, Marcie helped load the dishwasher and her mum insisted she did an hour's homework. Sighing, she went upstairs to do it all in double-quick time – she wanted to spend every minute possible with Comet!

When Marcie was sure her mum and dad were engrossed in watching the news on TV, she decided to risk nipping out to see Comet. She grabbed an apple from the fruit bowl on the kitchen table and quickly chopped it into bits before disappearing into the garden.

The sun was setting and streaks of

peach and salmon pink coloured the darkening sky. It was a glorious evening, and as Marcie jogged down the garden to the paddock, her heart began beating fast. She couldn't wait to see the magic pony again. But he wasn't standing in the paddock where she'd left him.

'Comet!' she called.

There was no answer. No handsome dapple-grey pony came galloping up the field. The door of the big old shed hung

open. Maybe Comet was inside. Marcie
went into the paddock to look.

But he wasn't in the shed, or behind it,
or anywhere else.

Marcie's high spirits took a dent as she
wondered whether Comet had changed
his mind about staying in the paddock.
Maybe he had grown tired of waiting
for her and gone to find someone else to
help him search for Destiny.

'Comet! Where are you?' she called
again, starting to get worried.

There was a faint rustling sound from
behind her.

'I am here, Marcie,' Comet nickered,
blowing warm breath into her hair.

Marcie spun round, a huge grin
spreading across her face. He smelt
wonderful – of grass and fresh air and

something sweet that was his own
magical scent. She threw her arms round
his neck and pressed her cheek to its silky
warmth.

'Oh, I'm so glad you came back!' she
burst out. 'I thought that maybe you'd left
because you didn't like it here.'

'I like it very much.' Comet's violet
eyes glowed with amusement. 'I simply
went to have a look around while I was
waiting for you. There might have been
traces of where Destiny has passed by.'

Lowering her arms, Marcie stepped
back. 'What sort of traces?' she asked
curiously.

'Wherever Destiny goes, she leaves a
trail of softly glowing hoof-prints that are
invisible to most people in your world,'
Comet told her, twitching his ears.

'Really?' Marcie said, amazed. 'Will I be able to see them?'

Comet nodded. 'But only if you are riding me or I am very close to you.'

Marcie knew he must be longing to find his twin sister, who was all alone and missing her family. 'I should be able to come and help you look for Destiny tomorrow. We usually go shopping together early on Saturdays. Mum and Dad always take hours and it can be dead boring. I'll make an excuse to stay here,' she decided.

Comet looked pleased. 'Thank you, Marcie.'

Marcie remembered the apple in her jeans pocket. 'I brought something for you.'

She took the slices out and offered

them to Comet on her flattened palm.
The magic pony stretched forward
and she felt his soft lips nuzzling her
cautiously as he picked up a piece of
apple.

He started crunching and in a few
moments he had eaten all the apple. 'That
was delicious. I like your human food.'

'Wait until you try carrots and
peppermints!' Marcie smiled, feeling a

rush of affection for her amazing new friend. 'See you in the morning then. Sweet dreams,' she called to him as she went towards the gate.

Chapter
FOUR

'Are you sure that you don't want to change your mind and come with us?' Marcie's dad asked the following morning as he picked up his car keys.

'Positive!' Marcie said firmly. 'You know I hate food shopping. I thought I'd ... um ... send Lara a really long email. I want to know how she's getting on at her new school, what her new house is like and if there are loads of good places to go out riding on Tramp.'

'Good idea, love. You and Lara can catch up on all the pony news, like you used to,' her dad said. His face clouded. 'I expect she'll be disappointed to hear that you won't be having a new pony after all.'

'Maybe at first, but she'll understand, like I do,' Marcie said brightly. 'Some things are better when you have to wait for them.' *Especially when you've already got a secret magic pony friend to keep you company!* she thought.

'I'm glad you're able to see things that way,' her dad said, looking happier.

'See you later!' Marcie waved as their car drove away and she closed the front door.

As she pulled on her riding boots and grabbed her hat, she made herself a promise to email Lara as soon as she got back from helping Comet look for Destiny.

Comet saw her coming towards the paddock and gave a whinny of welcome. The morning sun made his dapple-grey coat look like polished metal.

'Hi, Comet! We've got the whole morning to search for Destiny. Let's go, shall we?' she sang out.

Comet tossed his head with eagerness, his deep violet eyes flashing. 'Yes, Marcie, but I need to do one thing first.'

Marcie felt a warm prickling sensation flowing down to her fingertips as bright violet sparks bloomed in Comet's dapple-grey coat. There was a crackling sound and a flash of rainbow light, which quickly faded to reveal Comet standing there fully tacked-up.

'Wow! That's brilliant,' Marcie exclaimed at Comet's cleverness. He was full of surprises.

Comet pawed the ground. 'Climb on to my back, Marcie.'

Marcie checked that all the straps were tightened and then mounted. As the magic pony broke into a trot down to the far end of the paddock, Marcie moved in time to his strides. They reached the barred gate that opened straight into Willow Lane, and Marcie opened it and closed it behind them.

A few metres down the quiet winding lane, she turned Comet on to a track that led along the edge of a field and then to open farmland. Marcie and Lara had often ridden Tramp here. She knew all the best bridleways through the woods and which farmers allowed riders to cross their land.

'Let's go, Comet!' Marcie cried, nudging him on.

Comet snorted eagerly, pulling at his bit, and sprang forward into a gallop.

Marcie crouched low on his back,
her hair blowing in the warm breeze.
Excitement raced through her. Comet
was thrilling to ride, so smooth and
exciting, and his warm magic seemed to
spread around her, so that however fast
they went, she felt perfectly safe.

Comet almost flew along, his hooves
barely brushing the grass. His head turned

left and right as his sharp eyes searched
for any sign that Destiny had come this
way.

'Hold tight!' he told Marcie as he
surged up a slope that led to the crest
of a hill. At the top he paused, his mane
and tail stirring in the breeze, and then
plunged down the other side towards
some woods.

Marcie caught her breath, almost
laughing aloud with joy. Happiness filled
her. She loved nothing better in the
whole world than riding on a bright
sunny day.

Comet checked his stride and slowed as
they entered the shade of the trees.

Bright green ferns bordered the bridle
path on both sides and grew thickly
among the trees. They were so tall that

a dog or a very small pony could have hidden beneath them. Marcie peered into the undergrowth as they pressed on, keeping a lookout, but there was no sign of Destiny

After a thorough search, they emerged from the woods.

'I do not think she came this way,' Comet said, scanning the shallow ridge ahead of them, which was dotted with grazing sheep.

Marcie spotted two small ponies tethered in a field to one side. 'Look! Maybe Destiny is disguised as one of those!' she cried.

Comet nickered with renewed interest as he cantered over to investigate. But neither of the shaggy little ponies was Destiny. He trotted away sadly.

'I only hope that Destiny has found
a safe hiding place,' Comet whinnied.
'The dark horses are always watching and
waiting to steal our magic.'

'We'll find her. I know we will. There
are lots more places to search around here.
I'll show you.' Marcie patted his neck and
then clicked her tongue encouragingly.

They rode on, taking a circular route
that eventually brought them back
through the woods.

'I think we'd better make for home now,' Marcie decided reluctantly. 'Mum and Dad will be back soon.'

Comet nodded.

They retraced their steps, but skirted the bottom of the hill. The track came out further down Willow Lane. Facing them, Marcie could see the stone pillars that marked the large gateway of Blackberry Farm, which had been empty for ages.

She noticed that there were cars on the farmhouse drive and a woman was putting curtains up at an upstairs window. The stable block had been freshly painted.

On impulse, she reined in Comet and they stopped beside one of the stone pillars, out of sight of the main house.

'It looks like new people have moved

in,' she commented. 'I wonder what they're like.'

Just then, a large muscular brown horse burst out of an open stable door. Tossing its head, it laid back its ears and raced towards them.

Chapter
FIVE

'Quick, Comet! We have to stop that horse getting out!' Marcie cried. 'The busy main road runs along the bottom of Willow Lane!'

Comet stepped forward and stood side-on to block the gateway.

The brown horse snorted as it slewed to a halt half a metre away. Rolling its eyes, it reared up on to its back legs.

'Watch out! It's going to kick!' Marcie
warned, steeling herself for a painful blow
as the horse's flailing hooves came within
centimetres of hitting her leg. Though she
was more scared that Comet would be
hurt.

Pushing down on the stirrups she stood
up and waved her arms at the frightened
horse, hoping it would turn aside and not

try to bite or kick as it pushed past them.

Comet stood his ground. He turned his head to look at the brown horse and Marcie felt another tingling sensation flow down her fingers as violet sparks glowed in Comet's dapple-grey coat. A shimmering mist briefly surrounded the horse and then gradually faded along with every last violet spark.

The brown horse stood there, calm now. Its dark eyes were soft and kindly. Comet gave a friendly blow and reached out to touch noses gently with it.

'Well done, Comet!' Marcie dismounted and moved slowly towards the loose horse. Luckily it wore a head collar, so she reached up and grasped hold. 'Don't be scared now. It's OK, I won't hurt you,' she said reassuringly. To

her relief, it didn't throw up its head or
try to back away.

'You were very brave to try to stop that
horse,' Comet said to Marcie.

'I didn't really think about it. I couldn't
bear the idea of you being hurt. Anyway,
you were brave too,' she said, looking at
Comet adoringly. 'I reckon we saved each
other!'

'Oh, thank goodness. You've caught
her!'

A boy, who looked about twelve
years old, was running up to Marcie and
Comet. He had fair hair that flopped
forward on to his forehead and an open
friendly face.

A younger girl came pounding after
him. The girl drew level with the boy and
stood there, breathing hard.

'What's happening? Is Drift all right?'
she demanded, frowning.

The boy looked round at her. 'She's
fine. Don't panic, Sally. Luckily, this girl
caught her before she did herself any
damage.' He took a lead rope out of his
jeans pocket and clipped it on to the
brown horse's head collar.

'And we're fine too, thanks,' Marcie
said drily. It had been pretty scary to have

Drift run straight at her and Comet.

'Oh yeah. Sorry about that. Drift's a total sweetie, except when she's having one of her off days!' he said to Marcie with a narrow grin.

'Like today?' Marcie guessed, smiling. 'I'm Marcie Locket. I live just up the lane.'

'Hi, Marcie. I'm Ian Bale and this girl, who looks like she's just sucked a lemon, is my sister, Sally.'

'Very funny. Not!' Sally shot back at him.

She also had fair hair, held back from her face by a brown velvet hair band and there was a sprinkle of freckles on her cheeks. She looked about nine years old and would have been very pretty if she hadn't been scowling fiercely.

'You total idiot, Ian. You should have kept your eye on Drift,' Sally scolded her brother. 'You know what she can be like. Here, I'll take her.'

'Me? *You* left the stable door open!' Ian said.

'I did not!' Sally's cheeks flamed.

'Yes, you di– Oh, forget it,' Ian said, shrugging. He obviously couldn't be bothered to get into an argument in front of Marcie and Comet. Sighing, he handed her the leading rope. 'Suit yourself.'

His sister flashed him a triumphant grin and then clicked her tongue at Drift. Turning on her heel, she led the horse back towards the stables.

'Oh, by the way, thanks,' Sally murmured, not bothering to look back round at Marcie.

'No problem,' Marcie called after her.

Ian gave Marcie a wry grin. 'Don't mind Sally. She's a drama queen, but she never stays grumpy for long.' He ran an appreciative eye over Comet. 'He's a Connemara, isn't he? They're good all-rounders, aren't they? We used to have one. What's he called?'

'Comet,' Marcie told him.

'Hello, boy.' Ian put up his hand so Comet could nuzzle it. 'How long have you had him?' he asked Marcie.

'Not very long. Actually he's ... um ... on loan,' Marcie said vaguely, hoping to avoid awkward questions. 'I didn't know that anyone had moved into Blackberry Farm. How long have you been here?' she asked, quickly changing the subject.

'Just a couple of weeks,' Ian told her. 'I really like it here. I reckon there'll be lots of good places to ride.'

'There are,' Marcie agreed. 'I could show you and Sally some, if you like. Have you got any other horses or ponies besides Drift?'

'Yeah, we've got Rufus and Fiddler too. Would you like to come and meet them?'

'I'd love to –' Marcie began, but then remembered that she was supposed to be hurrying home before her parents returned from shopping. 'I can't now, though. I have to get back home.'

'OK, then,' Ian said easily. 'Why don't you come over tomorrow? Sally and I plan to go riding – if she's in a better mood, that is. You and Comet could come too and you can show us around.'

'Sounds great,' Marcie said, beaming. It would give her and Comet another chance to search for Destiny.

They arranged what time to meet up and then Marcie remounted Comet. 'Bye!' She waved to Ian before they rode up the lane.

'Ian was really nice, wasn't he?' Marcie said, once they were out of earshot.

Comet nodded. 'I like him too.'

'I'm not so sure about Sally, though,' Marcie commented. 'She seemed a bit grumpy. I hope Ian's right when he says she's usually OK. I'm looking forward to going riding with them tomorrow.'

Comet's deep violet eyes glowed under his long eyelashes. Marcie knew he was hoping he'd find Destiny.

Back home, she turned Comet out into the paddock. There was a small fountain of violet sparkles as the tack disappeared. Comet shook himself and then walked over to the trough for a long drink.

Marcie smiled at him. 'I'll come out and see you later and bring you some carrots,' she promised.

Inside the house, she quickly checked that her mum and dad weren't home and then dumped her riding boots and hat in the utility room. After fetching a cold drink, she went and sat at the family computer to write to Lara. She wished she could tell her all about the magical time she had been having with Comet!

Marcie was halfway through her email when she heard a car door slam. She looked out of the window to see her dad coming up the drive carrying bags of shopping.

The front door opened and then he stuck his head round the sitting-room door. 'Are you *still* on that PC, young lady? You must have an awful lot to tell Lara!' he teased.

Marcie beamed at him. 'I have!' *If only you knew*, she thought. 'Guess what? I've just met the two kids who've moved into Blackberry Farm: Sally and Ian Bale,' she told him, her enthusiasm running away with her. 'And they've got a horse and two ponies! I've got some new horsey friends and they live just down the road!'

Mr Locket looked puzzled. 'Really? Well, that *is* a bit of good luck, especially now that Lara isn't here. But how come you met Ian and Sally? I thought you said you'd be staying in the house. You know the rules about always letting us know where you are when you go out,' he said sternly.

Marcie realized her mistake. She thought fast. She could hardly tell her dad that she'd been perfectly safe because she was with Comet.

'Um . . . no, I didn't exactly go anywhere,' she fibbed. 'They . . . er . . . came past on their ponies and I just went outside on to the drive to talk to them. In fact, they've asked me to go riding with them tomorrow!'

Chapter
SIX

Marcie woke early the following morning
to find sunshine streaming through a gap
in the curtains.

'Yay! I'm going riding again on
Comet!' she said to herself as she leapt
out of bed and quickly dressed in jeans
and a T-shirt.

Her dad was already downstairs when
Marcie appeared. The delicious smell of

frying bacon met her as she opened the kitchen door.

'Dad! You're up early,' Marcie said, surprised. He usually liked a lie-in on Sundays.

He smiled, looking a bit weary. 'I didn't sleep very well with so much on my mind. So I thought I'd make breakfast. Bacon and egg sandwiches are on the menu, if you're interested.'

'You bet! Shall I cut the bread?' Marcie asked helpfully.

'Thanks, love. I expect you're looking forward to meeting up with your new friends. It's nice of them to invite you riding with them,' he commented.

'Yes, it is.' Marcie flipped her hair over her shoulder as she wielded the bread knife. The slices were a bit uneven, but her dad didn't seem to notice.

As soon as she'd finished breakfast, Marcie put on her riding kit and then said goodbye to her parents. 'See you later. I'll take the short cut across the paddock.'

She felt a thrill of excitement as she saw Comet standing with his head over the fence waiting for her. As she approached him, Comet curled his dark grey lips and greeted her with a neigh of welcome. He was already tacked-up and eager to go.

Marcie swung herself into the saddle and leaned over to pat his silky neck as they set off.

Ian and Sally were waiting for them in the stable yard. Ian was on a handsome chestnut pony with two white socks. Marcie guessed that this was Rufus. He waved as she and Comet rode through the front gates.

'Hi, Marcie!' Sally waved too. She was just mounting a pretty palomino.

'What a lovely pony!' Marcie said, pleased to see that Sally seemed in a better mood today.

Sally smiled, her blue eyes sparkling. 'Thanks. Fiddler's really sweet.'

'We usually take it in turns to exercise the ponies,' Ian told her, controlling Rufus as the chestnut pony sidestepped.

71

'Poor old Drift doesn't look too happy at being left behind.'

Marcie glanced to where the big brown horse was standing with her head over the paddock fence, watching them with mournful dark eyes. As Ian and Sally rode out on to Willow Lane in single file, Marcie gave Drift a last sympathetic look before following behind the others.

'I thought we could ride up to the old water tower on the hill. The view is great from up there,' Marcie said. It was also in the opposite direction to where she and Comet had already searched, which meant they would be able to check out a different area.

'I hope we'll find Destiny this time or some sign that she came this way,' she whispered to him as they reached the main road and waited at the crossing.

'I hope so too!' Comet replied.

Marcie froze, surprised that he had spoken aloud to her with Ian and Sally so close. But neither of them seemed to have noticed anything odd.

'Do not worry, Marcie,' Comet told her, as if he knew what she was thinking. 'Only you can hear me speaking.

Everyone else will just think I am neighing or snorting.'

'Cool!' Marcie whispered in reply, relaxing.

Once safely across the main road, Marcie took a side turn and led the way down a wide grassy track lined with hedgerow. The hawthorn was still covered with clusters of creamy flowers. Their sweet musty scent filled the air.

After a few kilometres the track opened out on to a sweep of hillside covered with sparse-looking grass. Marcie squeezed Comet into a gallop and Ian and Sally did the same. Rabbits dived for cover as the ponies sped past.

Ahead of them the ground rose steeply to where an old stone building topped the hill.

'Race you to the top!' Sally cried,
crouching low on Fiddler.

'You're on! Whoo-hoo!' Ian yelled,
urging Rufus forward.

Comet couldn't resist. He shot after the
ponies in a lightning burst of speed. In a
thunder of hooves, he streaked past them,
his dark grey tail flying out behind him
like a silken banner.

'Yay! Eat our dust!' Marcie yelled over
her shoulder.

Rufus and Fiddler stretched out and gave chase, but they couldn't match Comet's powerful stride. Marcie thought she noticed the shadow of a large horse spreading across the hillside as Comet raced past, but then it was gone, so she must have imagined it. They reached the brow of the hill, twenty lengths ahead of the others. She reined Comet in beside the water tower and they stood waiting for Ian and Sally.

'What kept you?' Marcie joked, as they rode up.

Ian laughed. 'I thought Rufus was fast, but Comet can *really* move!' he said admiringly.

'That was fun!' Sally said, her face glowing.

They sat in a line looking out at the

view over the green rolling hills. In the distance they could see a grey smudge, where the hills met the sky.

Marcie wondered where Destiny could be hiding in this wide-open space, broken only by isolated farms and the occasional sheep pen or shepherd's hut.

They continued on, riding more slowly and enjoying the fresh air and sunshine. In the fold of two hills, there was a fast-running stream and they stopped to let the ponies drink.

Marcie bent close to whisper to Comet. 'I haven't seen any signs that Destiny's been this way? Have you?'

Comet shook his head, twitching one ear disappointedly. 'Not yet.'

An hour later, Ian announced that he

was hungry and suggested they go back
to Blackberry Farm for lunch. And with
rumbling tummies, everyone agreed.

Back at the farm, Ian and Sally
untacked their ponies. Drift lifted her
head and nickered a welcome from the
paddock, seemingly very pleased not to
be by herself any longer. As the ponies all
seemed to be getting on well together,
Ian suggested that Marcie turn out
Comet with them.

Mrs Bale made an enormous and
hearty lunch, which they ate at a big
wooden table in the farmhouse kitchen.
Baked potatoes with cheese and salad,
followed by home-made scones with
strawberries and cream, all washed down
with lemonade.

After lunch, Sally took Marcie up to

her bedroom and excitedly showed her all the cups and rosettes she'd won on Fiddler. Marcie found herself having the best time she'd had since Lara had lived in her village. She would have liked to stop longer, but thought she'd better check that Comet was still happy at being left in the Bales' paddock with the other ponies.

Sally walked out to the stable yard with her. 'I had a great time today,' she said, a smile lighting up her pretty face.

'Me too,' Marcie said. 'Thanks for showing me your trophies and stuff.'

'That's OK. I've just got a brilliant new book about braiding manes and tails. You can borrow it sometime, if you like.'

'Sounds great. Thanks,' Marcie said warmly, pleased that she and Sally were now getting on so well. Maybe she'd ask her to come over soon and they could watch her favourite *Black Beauty* DVD.

Ian was in the tack room, hanging up clean bridles and folding horse blankets. 'I'll do this all by myself, then, shall I?' he teased, rolling his eyes at his sister.

'Yeah! Why don't you?' Sally gave him a playful shove, but began helping him.

Marcie grinned. Those two were a double act! Shaking her head slowly, she walked the few metres to the paddock.

'Are you ready to go home now?' she whispered to Comet.

'Yes. I thought I might go out searching for Destiny again,' Comet told her. 'But I do not think you should come with me, as I sensed the dark horses' presence earlier.'

Marcie felt a prickle of concern. So she hadn't been imagining things – that dark shadow was real. Would Comet's magic be strong enough to protect him from his enemies when he was so far from home?

Her mind was filled by this worrying thought as she led him out and let the paddock gate shut itself behind her with a soft click.

Chapter
SEVEN

As it was growing dark, Marcie slipped
down the garden to check that Comet
had returned after his latest search.

To her relief he was there, his
dapple-grey coat gleaming softly in
the moonlight. Her heart swelled with
happiness and pride as she looked at him.
She didn't think she'd ever get over the
incredible feeling of being friends with a

magic pony.

'Greetings, Marcie,' Comet snorted softly.

'I was worried about you,' she admitted. 'What would happen if the dark horses found you while you were looking for Destiny?' she asked him.

'Before I came here I looked into the Stone of Power to see where Destiny was. Its magic still gives me some protection,' he told her.

Reassured, Marcie gave him some pieces of carrot from her pocket. Comet crunched them up eagerly. She spent a few more minutes with him, saying goodnight, and then hurried back indoors before she was missed.

Mr Locket had just finished on the computer. Marcie asked if she could use it and emailed Lara to tell her about her ride with Ian and Sally. She didn't mention Comet, but said that she'd borrowed Drift to ride. She sent the message and after a couple of minutes, Lara emailed back to say that she'd love to meet Ian, Sally and their ponies when she came to visit.

Marcie signed out and then logged off. She was feeling happier than she had for some time as she went upstairs to read for

A Special Wish

a while before going to bed. But she had
only just opened her book, when a loud
knocking sounded on the front door.

She sat up, frowning. Who could it be
at this late hour?

Marcie came out of her bedroom as
her dad answered the door.

Ian's panicky voice floated up to her.
'Is Marcie there? All the ponies have
escaped! Can she come and help us look
for them?'

'Oh no!' Marcie flung herself down the
stairs. 'What happened? How did they get
out?'

Ian avoided her eyes. 'Um . . . never
mind that now. Sally's already out looking
for them with Mum and Dad. I've come
to ask you to help, because you know the
area better than we do.'

'I'll just grab a torch!' Marcie turned to her mum and dad. 'It's OK if I go, isn't it?'

They nodded. 'Of course you must help, but you can't go out in the middle of the night by yourself,' her dad said.

'We'll come too,' her mum decided.

After grabbing coats, boots and torches, Marcie, Ian and her mum and dad set out. They walked round the road and turned into the top of Willow Lane. Sally and her mum came hurrying up to them.

'Any sign of the ponies?' Ian asked his sister.

In the torchlight Sally's face looked pale and drawn. She shook her head. 'Dad thinks they might have cut across the fields opposite. He's gone to look.' Her voice broke on a sob. 'Oh, I hope they have. I can't bear to think about them getting out on to the main road . . .'

Marcie went to put a comforting hand on Sally's arm.

The other girl twisted away distractedly. 'Don't touch me!' she snapped.

Marcie tried not to feel hurt. Sally must be so upset that she hardly knew what she was saying. Marcie didn't blame her. She knew she'd be half mad with worry if anything happened to Comet.

Comet! He would find the missing ponies in no time, but how could she get away from the others and go to ask him for his help?

'I'll . . . um . . . check on this side,' Marcie decided on impulse. 'Dad? Why don't you and mum fetch the car and meet me down at the bottom field. The one with the gate that leads out on to the main road.'

'It makes sense to split up,' her mum agreed. 'And Marcie knows these fields like the back of her hand.' She turned to Marcie. 'Don't take any risks, love. If you see any sign of the ponies, stand still and keep flashing your torch on and off until someone comes to help you.'

'I will,' Marcie promised, already pointing the torch to light her way as she walked over the cattle grid into the first field.

She crossed her fingers, hoping that none of the others would follow. Luckily, Ian went off with Sally and their mum, while Marcie's parents headed for their garage. Marcie was about to double back and head for Comet's paddock, when her fingers began to tingle and Comet himself appeared beside her in a cloud of shimmering rainbow mist.

'Comet! What are you doing here? I was just about to come and look for you!'

'I heard all the voices and guessed what had happened. Hurry! Climb on my back, Marcie! Do not worry. I have used my magic to make you invisible too when you are riding me.'

Marcie mounted. She twisted her hands

into his dark grey mane and held on tight.
'I'm ready!'

Comet sped away, moving as fast as
the wind. A protective bubble of rainbow
sparkles surrounded Marcie, keeping her
safe on top of Comet's back. One. Two.
Three. The fields rushed past in a magical
blur. There was no sign of the ponies.

Down in the bottom field, Comet raced alongside the tall hedgerow towards the gate. They had to find the ponies before they reached it and were spooked by the traffic that lay in the road beyond. Comet sped on, his flashing hooves eating up the ground.

Suddenly, Marcie spotted three shadowy fast-moving shapes in the distance.

'Look there's Drift, Rufus and Fiddler!' she gasped. 'Thank goodness they're all together.'

'I see them too,' Comet neighed.

Leaping forward in another dizzying burst of speed, he easily closed the distance between them. Comet rode up alongside the terrified ponies. Marcie's fingers tingled again as he sent out an invisible spray of violet sparks that settled on them like soft rain.

The runaway ponies gradually slowed to a trot and then a walking pace and finally they stopped, their sides heaving.

Marcie was still worried. Any one of the ponies could get scared by a sudden noise and bolt again. And the gate to the main road was horribly close.

'Do you think you could use your magic to make them follow you?' she asked urgently.

Comet nodded. 'I have an idea. This way they will get to safety more quickly.'

There was another violet flash of Comet's sparkly magic, and rainbow shimmers whirled around them all. Marcie felt the air whistle past her ears as they all found themselves flying through

the night with the stars twinkling above
them. There was a slight jolt as Comet's
hooves touched down further up the
field. The other ponies were safely beside
him.

'Wow! You were amazing, Comet!'
Marcie said, dismounting.

'I am glad I could help.'

She was reaching up to hug him, when
she felt him stiffen and lean down to stare
at the grass.

Marcie looked down too. In front of them both and stretching away up the hill was a faint line of softly glowing violet hoof-prints.

'Destiny! She came this way!' Comet whinnied excitedly.

Marcie felt a pang. Did that mean that he was leaving, right now? 'Are . . . are you going after her?' she asked anxiously.

Comet shook his head. 'No. The trail is cold. But it proves Destiny was here,' he said, his eyes glowing with fresh hope. 'When she is very close, I will be able to hear her hoof-beats. And then I may have to leave suddenly, without saying goodbye.'

Marcie bit her lip as she realized she had secretly been hoping that he might stay forever. 'Couldn't you and

Destiny live here with me and share your paddock?' she asked hopefully.

'No, Marcie, that is not possible. We must return to our family on Rainbow Mist Island,' Comet explained gently.

Marcie swallowed hard, feeling tears well up. 'I guess I knew that really,' she admitted. She forced herself to smile as she decided not to think about Comet leaving and to enjoy every single moment she had with him.

Just then a car swung off the main road and pulled into the gateway. Its headlights streamed into the field on to Marcie, Comet and the ponies. Marcie felt herself tense and then relax again as she remembered that Comet was invisible to everyone except her.

'I am not needed now. I will see you tomorrow, Marcie.' Comet disappeared in a final shower of violet sparkles that glistened as they fell around Marcie's feet.

'Marcie! You've found them!' Her mum and dad had opened the gate and were walking towards her.

Moments later, Ian, Sally and Mr and Mrs Bale appeared at the top of the field, their torch-beams wobbling as they came running towards the Lockets from the opposite direction.

'There they are! It's our ponies!' Sally cried, dashing forward.

Fiddler nickered softly as she saw her. Sally flung her arms round the palomino's neck and burst into tears of relief.

'It's OK, Sally. Fiddler isn't injured. They're all fine,' Marcie said reassuringly. She wished she could have told the other girl about how brilliant Comet had been, but of course, she never would.

Sally turned on Marcie, her face twisted in anger. 'No thanks to you! It was your fault in the first place! You left the paddock gate unlatched. That's why the ponies escaped!'

Chapter
EIGHT

Marcie blinked at Sally in shock and
dismay.

'I . . . I didn't. I closed the paddock gate
after I let Com–' she began and broke off
in confusion, as she remembered that she
couldn't mention the magic pony in front
of her parents. They had no idea that he
even existed.

Sally's lip curled. 'You obviously didn't

bother to check that it was fastened properly. Don't try and wriggle out of this. You could at least say sorry!'

'I would apologize, but I honestly don't think I left the gate open,' Marcie said reasonably.

But Sally was too wound up to listen. 'I don't believe you! Stay away from me. Do you hear?' she shouted. She whirled round and stomped away.

Marcie watched her go, speechless. 'Ian. You believe me, don't you?' She turned to him, hoping that he would listen to her.

But he shrugged and looked embarrassed. 'I . . . I don't know, Marcie. Leave it for now. You can't get through to Sally when she's like this,' he said. He turned to his dad. 'Let's get the ponies home.'

Mr Bale nodded. He thanked Marcie's mum and dad for helping to search for the ponies.

Mrs Bale turned to Marcie. 'Whatever did happen, no harm's done. Don't worry about it now. Let's all go home,' she suggested.

'Everything will seem clearer after a night's sleep,' Mrs Locket agreed. 'Come on, Marcie. We'll all drive back.'

Marcie's heart was heavy as she trudged through the gate and went towards the car with her parents. 'I don't get it. Why's everyone blaming me?' she gulped, close to tears.

'They're tired and upset,' her dad soothed. 'I suggest you go and see Ian and Sally when they've had a chance to calm down.'

'It won't do any good. I know what Sally's like. She hates me now,' Marcie said miserably.

Their promising new friendship looked like it was over before it had really got started.

Over the next few days, Marcie racked her brains, trying to remember whether she had left the Bales' paddock gate open.

She was talking to Comet one morning before she left for school. 'I remember that I was worried about you meeting those horrible dark horses when I let you out of the Bales' paddock. Maybe I wasn't concentrating and I left the gate off the latch. If I'm honest, I'm not even sure any more.'

Comet's deep violet eyes softened. 'Even if you did, it was not done deliberately.'

'Try telling Sally that,' Marcie said sadly. 'I've called round twice after school *and* phoned, but she won't even talk to me. She's my best friend here now that Lara's moved away. No one loves ponies as much as we do at school! Even Ian's only just about speaking to me, but I'm sure he's just being polite. I know he secretly

blames me for letting the ponies escape.
I feel awful!'

Comet leaned towards her and huffed
out a soft warm breath. 'You are a kind
person and good friend.'

Marcie felt herself calming down as
she stroked his velvety dark-grey muzzle.
'Thanks for believing in me. You're the
best friend anyone could have,' she said
fondly.

Comet fell silent and his ears swivelled thoughtfully.

'What?' Marcie asked.

'Do you remember the day we met Ian and Sally at the farm gateway?'

Marcie nodded. How could she forget? 'You stopped Drift from hurting us and galloping out into Willow Lane, didn't you? Sally and Ian were squabbling about who'd left the stable door open.'

'That is right.' Comet's mane stirred in the breeze. 'Did they not also say that Drift could be difficult?'

'Yes,' Marcie agreed, trying to remember exactly what the Bales had said about the big brown horse. 'I got the impression that she likes escaping and running off.'

'That is what I thought.' Comet

snorted in satisfaction, his eyes twinkling mysteriously.

Marcie frowned, still puzzled. What was Comet getting at?

'I think you should go and see Ian and Sally again,' Comet decided, swishing his tail.

'Really? I'm not sure it would do any good,' Marcie said doubtfully, but she trusted Comet's judgement. 'I will, if you think I should.'

Comet nodded. 'I do, Marcie. Friendship is important. Is it not worth fighting for?'

'I guess it is,' Marcie agreed. 'I'll give it one more try and this time I'm not leaving until Sally agrees to talk to me. We'll go over to Blackberry Farm as soon as I get home after school. OK?'

Comet nodded, his eyes shining with wisdom.

Marcie was so nervous about their plan to go and see Sally and Ian that she could hardly concentrate in class.

Somehow she managed to get through her schoolwork. Luckily, they were concentrating on their projects. Marcie's was about heavy horses and their lives, so she found herself enjoying writing a page about shire horses. It was a surprise when the bell went for the end of lessons and she could rush out to meet her mum.

'You seem a bit more cheerful,' Mrs Locket said as she parked the car on their drive. 'Have you made things up with Ian and Sally?'

'Not yet. But I'm working on it!'

She changed out of her uniform and was about to go out to Comet when the house phone rang.

Her mum picked it up.

Marcie heard her say, 'When did this happen?' *It's your Dad*, Mrs Locket mouthed at her silently.

Marcie crossed her fingers and toes for good luck as she waited for her mum to put the phone down. *Please, please let it be good news*, she prayed.

Mrs Locket took a deep breath and stood with her hand on her chest.

Marcie almost exploded with impatience. 'Mu-um! What's going on?'

'I can hardly believe it myself,' her mum said, blinking dazedly. 'Your dad's just been offered a new job, much better than his present one. He starts next week.

It pays a lot more than he's been getting. So I think you can start looking at ponies for sale.'

'Really? Yay! That's fantastic! Good for Dad!' Marcie squealed. She grabbed her mum and they did a triumphant little dance up and down the hall.

She was going to get her pony and Comet would have a new friend to share the paddock with! She couldn't wait to email Lara and tell her the fabulous news, not mentioning Comet, of course. But first, she was going to Blackberry Farm.

'I'm going to make Sally see what she's missing by not being my friend,' she told her mum determinedly.

'Good for you, love. That's the way. It might be tough to get her to talk to you, though. Do you want me to come with you?'

'No. I have to do this on my own,' Marcie said firmly, already halfway out of the door. 'I won't be long.'

At the paddock, she told Comet the good news about her dad's new job.

His intelligent eyes shone. 'That is

wonderful, Marcie. What sort of pony would you like?'

'A Connemara, of course! What else?' Marcie said immediately. 'Everything's starting to go right now. It would be just perfect if Ian and Sally wanted to be friends with me again.'

Comet didn't reply. He tossed his head and in a flash and a cloud of violet sparkles he was fully tacked-up. 'Climb on my back, Marcie!' he neighed.

As they rode out on to Willow Lane, Marcie's bright self-confidence wavered. What if Sally still wasn't prepared to listen to her?

They had reached the curve in the lane, just before Blackberry Farm, when Marcie heard a sound she had been longing for and dreading at the same time.

The hollow sound of hooves galloping overhead.

'Destiny!' Comet veered off into the nearby field, following the magical hoof-beats, which sounded louder and closer. Panting with excitement, he halted briefly beside a hedgerow.

'You must get down now, Marcie,' he told her gently.

Marcie dismounted. She knew that this time he was leaving. Her heart ached with sadness, but she knew she would have to be very strong.

There was a violet flash and a twinkling rainbow mist floated down around Comet. He stood there in his true form, a dapple-grey pony no longer, but a magnificent magic pony with a noble head, cream coat and spreading golden wings. His golden mane and tail flowed down in shimmering silken strands.

'Comet!' Marcie gasped. She had almost forgotten how beautiful he was.

'I hope you catch Destiny. Good luck! I'll never forget you!' she said, her voice breaking.

Comet's deep violet eyes clouded over for a moment with sadness. 'Farewell, young friend. Ride well and true,' he said in a deep musical voice.

There was a final violet flash of light and a silent burst of rainbow sparkles that showered down round Marcie in crystal droplets and tinkled as they hit the grass.

Comet spread his wings and soared upwards. He faded and was gone.

Marcie gulped back tears, hardly able to believe that this had happened so fast. Something glittered on the grass. It was a single shimmering gold wing-feather. Reaching down, she picked it up. It tingled against her palm as it faded to a cream colour. She slipped it into her pocket, knowing that she would treasure it always as a reminder of the wonderful adventure she had shared with the magic pony.

As Marcie stepped back out on to Willow Lane, Sally waved at her from the farm gate.

'Marcie! Come here,' she cried. 'I've got something to show you!'

Quickly wiping her eyes, Marcie followed. Sally didn't seem to be quite as angry with her right now. Marcie was puzzled.

Ian was standing by the stable door, just out of sight of Fiddler, Rufus and Drift in the nearby paddock. He gestured to Marcie to be quiet. 'Watch this,' he whispered, pointing at Drift.

The brown horse pricked her ears. She walked up to the gate. Leaning her weight against the catch, Drift used her teeth to spring it, so that the gate swung slowly open. Ian quickly rushed forward, closed it again and slipped a loop of rope over it, before she could escape.

Marcie blinked in astonishment. 'So that's how all the ponies got out!'

'Yes. It was Drift. She can open doors and gates. I'm so sorry that I blamed you. I've been such a muppet, haven't I?' Sally said.

Marcie realized that Comet had worked all this out. This was his final gift to her before he had to leave forever.

'Who cares?' Grinning widely, she gave Sally a big hug. 'I'm just glad we can be friends again!'

You were right, Comet! Marcie said silently. *Friendship is worth fighting for.* Wherever he was, she knew that his

deep violet eyes would be shining with
approval.

Out Now

Magic Ponies

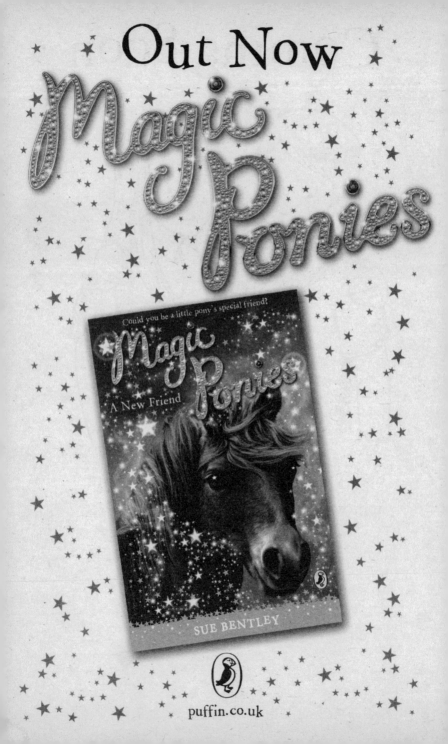

Could you be a little pony's special friend?

Magic Ponies

A New Friend

SUE BENTLEY

Coming Soon

Magic Ponies

A Twinkle of Hooves

Showjumping Dreams

Magic Puppy

A New Beginning
9780141323503

Muddy Paws
9780141323510

Cloud Capers
9780141323527

Star of the Show
9780141323534

Party Dreams
9780141323794

A Forest Charm
9780141323800

Twirling Tails
9780141323817

School of Mischief
9780141323824

Snowy Wishes
9780141323831

Classroom Princess
9780141324791

Friendship Forever
9780141324784

Sparkling Skates
9780141324777

Sunshine Shimmers
9780141324760

Spellbound at School
9780141324753

Coming Soon

The Perfect Secret
9780141324746

A little puppy
a sprinkling of magic,
a forever friend

Magic Ponies

Win a Magic Ponies goody bag!

Golden feathers from Comet's wings are falling out as he desperately tries to find his twin sister, Destiny, who is still lost in our world! The feathers carry a secret message for Destiny.

Two words from the message can be found in magic golden feathers hidden in *A New Friend* and *A Special Wish*.

To help save Destiny from danger, find the hidden words and put them together to complete the message. Send it in to us and each month we will put every correct message in a draw and pick out one lucky winner to receive a whole stable of Magic Ponies goodies!

Send your secret message, name and address on a postcard to:

Magic Ponies competition

Puffin Books

80 Strand

London WC2R 0RL

Please help Comet save his sister!

Good luck!

puffin.co.uk

It all started with a Scarecrow

Puffin is well over sixty years old.
Sounds ancient, doesn't it? But Puffin has never been
so lively. We're always on the lookout for the next big
idea, which is how it began all those years ago.

Penguin Books was a big idea from the mind of
a man called Allen Lane, who in 1935 invented
the quality paperback and changed the world.
**And from great Penguins, great Puffins grew,
changing the face of children's books forever.**

The first four Puffin Picture Books were hatched in 1940 and the
first Puffin story book featured a man with broomstick arms called
Worzel Gummidge. In 1967 Kaye Webb, Puffin Editor, started the
Puffin Club, promising to **'make children into readers'**.
She kept that promise and over 200,000 children became
devoted Puffineers through their quarterly installments of
Puffin Post, which is now back for a new generation.

Many years from now, we hope you'll look back and
remember Puffin with a smile. **No matter what your age
or what you're into, there's a Puffin for everyone.**
The possibilities are endless, but one thing is for sure:
whether it's a picture book or a paperback, a sticker book
or a hardback, **if it's got that little Puffin
on it – it's bound to be good.**